I LOVE YOU MORE

This book belongs to ___June___

*I always love a
good book, especially
when you read
with someone you
love. All my love,
Auntie Gigi*

This one is for all those I love

for infinity and beyond

Library of Congress Cataloging-in-Publication Data

Cooley, Judy.
 I love you more / Judy Cooley.
     p. cm.
  Summary: At bedtime, a young girl and her father compete in saying how much they love one another.
  ISBN 1-59038-432-6 (hardbound : alk. paper)
  [1. Fathers and daughters--Fiction. 2. Bedtime--Fiction.] I. Title.

PZ7.C77661I 2005
[E]--dc22   2004030100

Printed in China   18961
R. R. Donnelley and Sons, Shenzhen

10   9   8   7   6   5   4

I LOVE YOU MORE

Written and Illustrated by
JUDY COOLEY

SHADOW MOUNTAIN

To June—

You are loved
evefinity + one!

The other night, Daddy came in to tuck me into bed. When he had the covers fixed all nice and cozy, he kissed me on the forehead. I said, "I love you, Daddy."

"I love you too, princess," he said.

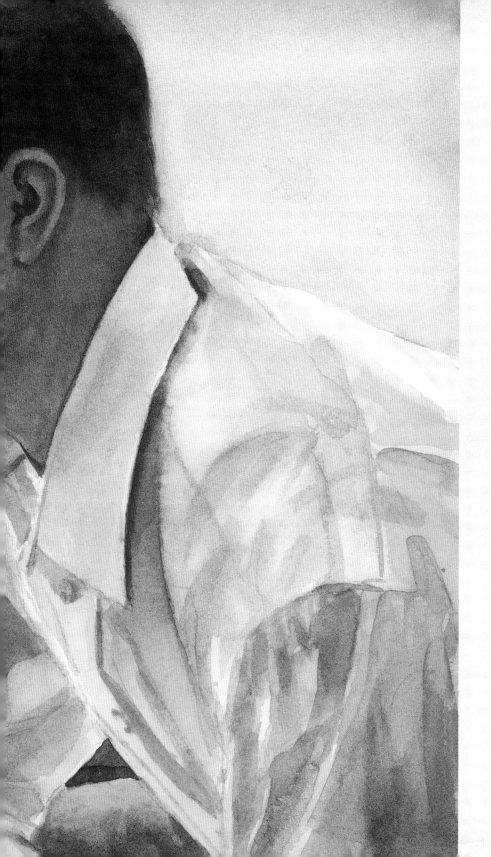

G uess what?" I said. "I love you three."

That made me giggle.

Daddy laughed too. "Well, then, I love you

four," he said.

I love you, Daddy, more than there were friends at my tea party," I said.

L et's see," said Daddy. "I love you more than there are colors in your sidewalk chalk."

🦋 🦋 🦋

I quickly said, "I love you more than there are pumpkins in Maggie's pumpkin patch."

Daddy laughed again. "That's a lot," he said, "but . . ."

I love you more than there are lilies on Teacup Lake. Top *that!*"

I love you more than there are dandelions
in our field," I said. I've picked *lots* of
dandelions, so I knew that was a bunch.

I thought I was winning until Daddy said,

"I love you more than there are lilacs on

Grandma's trees in the spring."

Daddy was smiling, but I was smiling bigger. I said, "I love you more than there are snowflakes in the first storm of the winter."

But Daddy didn't give up very easily. He said, "I love you more than there are grains of sand on the beach."

What could be more than that?
I thought and thought, until I had the best
idea ever. I said, "I love you more than
there are stars in the night sky." I knew I
had won for sure.

Ut you know how daddies are. Daddy smiled and said, "I love you more than infinity."

"What's that?" I asked. "I've never seen an infinity before."

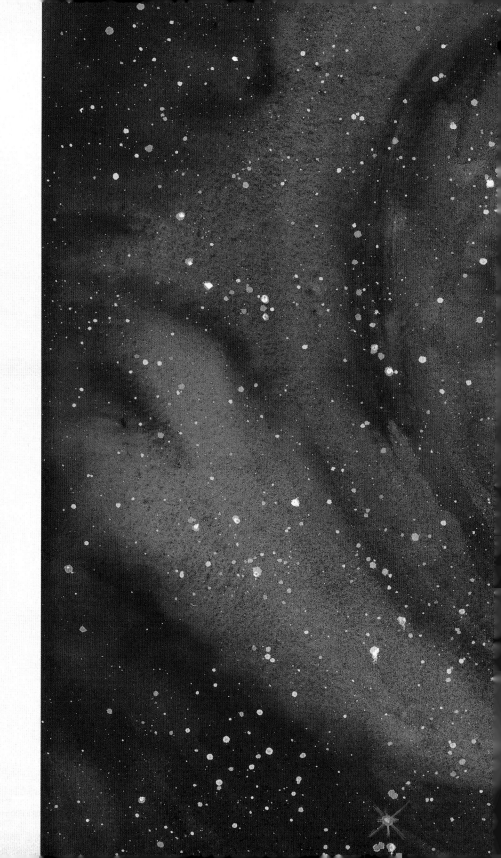

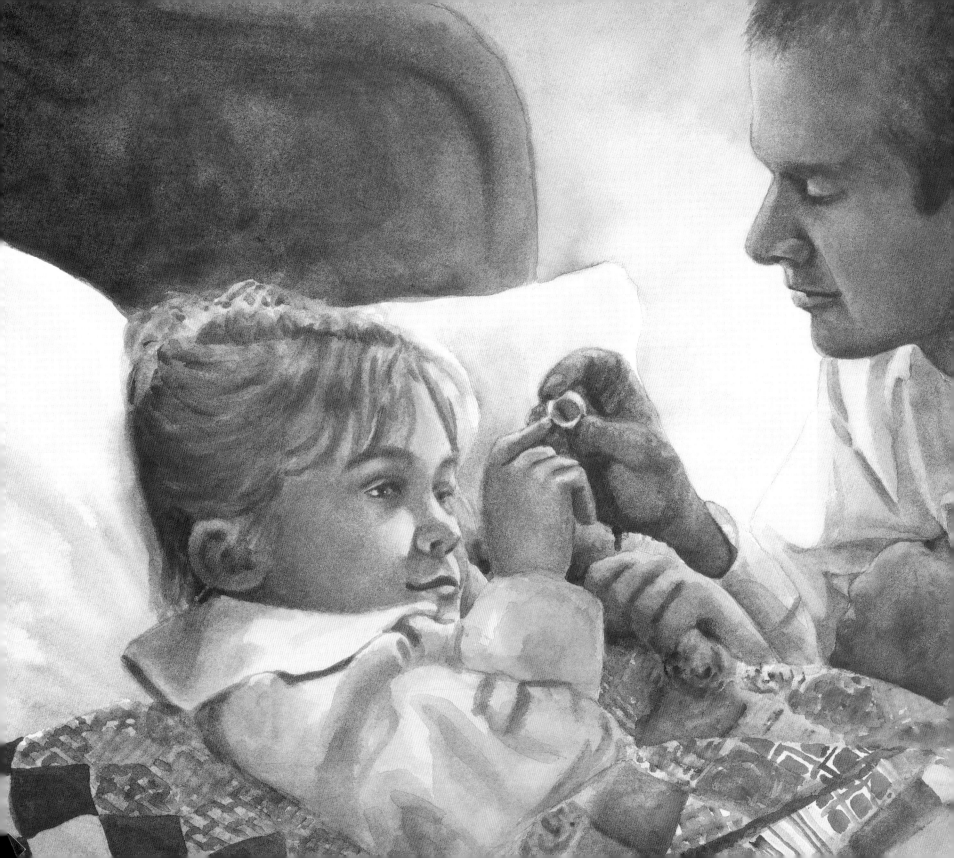

Daddy took off his wedding ring and

said, "See how a circle has no beginning or end?

It never stops, just like numbers and space.

They go on and on forever. That's infinity.

That's how much I love you!"

I win," Daddy said, giving me a great big hug. Then suddenly I thought of something. "No wait! *I win*, Daddy, because I love you infinity plus one!"

. . . and they lived happily *infinity* after.